Ben had
a balloon.

Ben's balloon
went up.
"Bye, Ben,"
said his sister.

Come Back, Ben

by
Ann Hassett
and
John Hassett

I Like to Read®

Holiday House / New York

For Bob

I LIKE TO READ is a registered trademark of Holiday House, Inc.

Copyright © 2013 by Ann Hassett and John Hassett.
All Rights Reserved
HOLIDAY HOUSE is registered in the U.S. Patent and Trademark Office.
Printed and Bound in April 2013 at Tien Wah Press, Johor Bahru, Johor, Malaysia.
The text typeface is Report School.
The artwork was created with cut paper and ink.
www.holidayhouse.com
First Edition
1 3 5 7 9 10 8 6 4 2

Library of Congress Cataloging-in-Publication Data
Hassett, Ann (Ann M.)
Come back, Ben / by Ann & John Hassett. — 1st ed.
p. cm. — (I like to read)
Summary: A balloon takes Ben on an adventure.
ISBN 978-0-8234-2599-0 (hardcover)
I. Hassett, John. II. Title.
PZ7.H2784Co 2013
[E] —dc23
2011049310

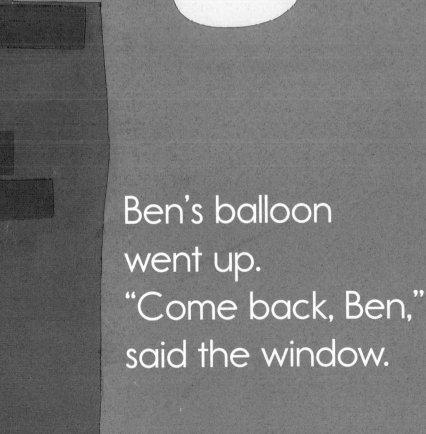

Ben's balloon
went up.
"Come back, Ben,"
said the window.

Ben's balloon
went up.

"Come back, Ben,"
said the bees.

Ben's balloon
went up.
"Come back, Ben,"
said the tree.

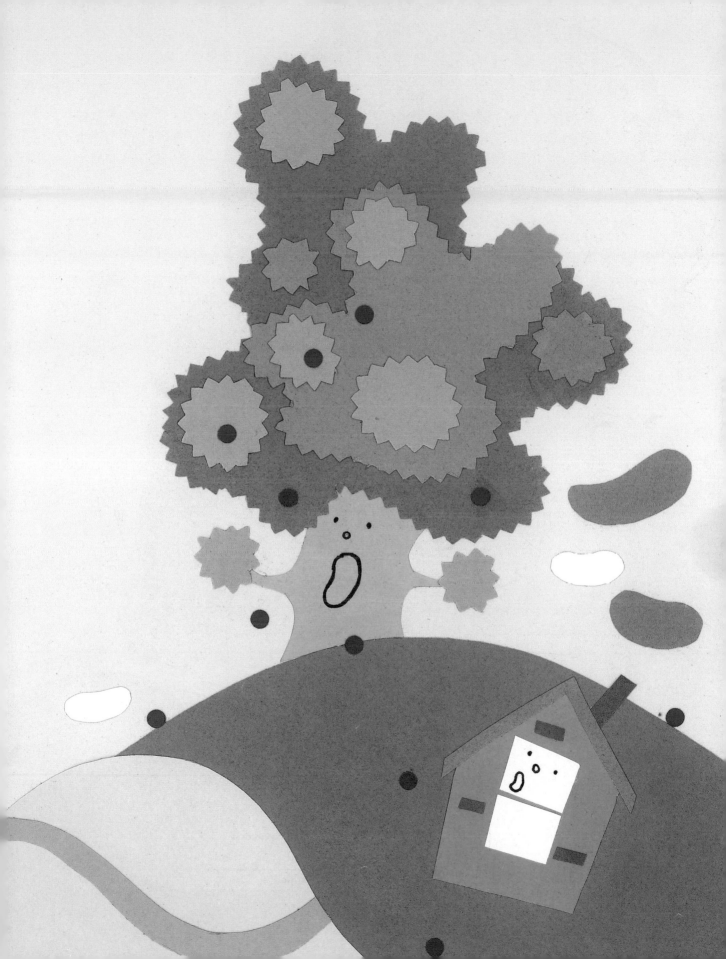

Ben's balloon
went up.
"Come back, Ben,"
said the kite.

Ben's balloon
went up.

"Come back, Ben,"
said the big hill.

Ben's balloon
went up.

"Come back, Ben,"
said the rain.
"Come back, Ben,"
said the rainbow.

Ben's balloon went up
to the moon.
"Hi, Ben,"
said the moon.

Ben put moon rocks
in his pockets.

"Good-bye, Ben,"
said the moon.
Ben's balloon
went down.

Ben's balloon went up.
"Bye, balloon," said Ben.

"Bye, Ben,"
said his sister.